Will   Irma   Taranee   Cornelia   Hay Lin

ADVENTURES

Heartbreak Island

© 2005 Disney Enterprises, Inc.
Text copyright © 2002 by Lene Kaaberbol
W.I.T.C.H. Will Irma Taranee Cornelia Hay Lin
is a trademark of Disney Enterprises, Inc.
Volo® is a registered trademark of Disney Enterprises, Inc.
Volo/Hyperion Books for Children are imprints of
Disney Children's Book Group, L.L.C.

Printed in Singapore
First U.S. edition
1 3 5 7 9 10 8 6 4 2

This book is set in 11.5/16 Hiroshige Book.
ISBN 0-7868-0981-7
Visit www.clubwitch.com

ADVENTURES

Heartbreak Island

By Lene Kaaberbol

VOLO

an imprint of
HYPERION BOOKS FOR CHILDREN
New York

*O*nce, long ago, when the universe was young, spirits and creatures lived under the same sky. There was only one world, only one vast realm, governed by the harmonies of nature. But evil entered the world, and found its place in the hearts and minds of spirits and creatures alike, and the world shattered into many fragments. The realm was split between those who wished for peace and those who lived to gain power over others and cause them pain. To guard and protect what was good in the worlds, the mighty stronghold of Candracar was raised in the middle of infinity.

There, a congregation of powerful spirits and creatures keep vigilance; chief among them is the Oracle. His wisdom is much needed; at times,

Candracar is all that keeps evil from entering where it should have no place.

There is also the Veil. A precious barrier between good and evil, guarded by unlikely girls.

Irma has power over water. Taranee can control fire. Cornelia has all the powers of earth. Hay Lin holds the lightness and the freedom of air. And Will, the Keeper of the Heart of Candracar, holds a powerful amulet in which all of the natural elements meet to become energy, pure and strong.

Together they are W.I.T.C.H.—five Guardians of the Veil. And the universe needs them. . . .

1

I remember that Friday very well. All day long I had a hard time concentrating on anything at school. I was too excited about my Friday night plans. No, I didn't have a romantic date! The Hawks were playing in Heatherfield that night. My favorite basketball team in the country was playing in my town! And I was going.

As I waited for my friend Will outside of school, I thought about having courtside seats and watching the hottest game of the season. The Hawks were playing their rivals, the Silver Bay Giants. I was hoping my favorite Hawk, Seb Caine, would be playing. He had an injury from a few weeks ago, but I was hoping that he would be fine for the Friday night game. Caine was such a *smooth* player.

"Taranee?" Will said, interrupting my thoughts. "You can let go now."

I looked down at the bicycle I was holding. The bike was bright red. It was Will's bike.

Will gave me an odd look. "Taranee, are you feeling okay?"

"Sure," I said and gave Will her bike. Then I jumped on my own bike, ready for the ride home.

"You look kind of out of it," Will said. "And Hay Lin said you got a math problem wrong in class. I've never seen you get a wrong answer in class, especially math. It's almost like . . . like you were in another world."

As Guardians of the Veil, we're used to being in other worlds. Will is the W of W.I.T.C.H. I'm the T. Along with our friends Irma, Cornelia, and Hay Lin, we go to different worlds to fight evildoers and other folks who work against the good power of Candracar. Will was right—I was in another world at that moment. But it was the world of basketball, where the only evildoer was the star forward on the opposing team.

"The Hawks are playing in town tonight," I told her.

"*Oh,*" said Will, in a tone of absolute understanding. She knows me very well. Besides being a fellow Guardian, she is also my best friend.

"Are you going to the game?" she asked.

I nodded enthusiastically. "Peter got us some really great tickets."

"Nice brother you've got," Will shouted after me as we started to pedal away from school.

"Yeah," I called back to her. "Peter is the best."

However, when I got home there was no big brother waiting for me. The only thing that greeted me was the answering machine.

"Hey, Taranee. Sorry I'm not there yet. Could you call me back, please? Something's come up. Don't worry, we'll still make the game, but call me, okay? I'll leave my cell phone on."

I felt a small flutter of unease. *Something's come up.* I was willing to bet my Hawks ticket that that *something* was Suzanne with the supermodel good looks. I should have hated her, except she also happened to be supernice. *And* smart. Maybe I hated her anyway. Nobody should have all that and my big brother, too.

I picked up the phone and called Peter.

"Hi, Peter," I said when I heard his voice. I began playing with the beads in my hair.

"Oh, hi, Taranee. Sorry about this, but . . . well, I promised I'd take Suzanne to her dad's, so could we meet outside the game? Take the bus, I'll pay you back when I see you. Okay?"

"I guess," I said. I was not happy about taking the bus, but at least he wasn't canceling our night at the game. That would be worse.

"Taranee," he said. "I'm really sorry."

He did sound sorry. I sighed. "Yeah, okay. Don't be late. I want to see the Hawks warm-up."

"Totally!" Peter said. "You're the best. See you soon."

"Yeah," I said with another sigh as he ended the call.

I put on my green-and-yellow Hawks jacket and my green-and-yellow Hawks scarf and my green-and-yellow Hawks cap and my boots with the green-and-yellow laces. I even changed the beads in my hair to Hawks colors. I looked like a serious fan!

I took the bus to the Dome, home of the Heatherfield Hawks. And I waited. And waited. And waited.

€ € ◮ ◉ ◖

At first, I wasn't really mad. Peter is not usually late, and never *really* late. People went streaming through the gates, some wearing green-and-yellow caps, others sporting the sky blue and gray of the Silver Bay Giants.

Gradually, the stream thinned to a trickle. Then there was only me and the gatekeeper, and just to make my mood even gloomier, rain began to fall. From inside, I could hear the muted roar of the crowd and the blare of the loudspeakers as the names of the players were announced. I was missing warm-up. At that moment, I was steaming mad. I wouldn't have been surprised if my glasses had gotten all fogged up from my own heated anger!

"You coming in, miss?" the gatekeeper asked.

I looked around. Peter was still missing.

"I have a ticket," I said desperately. "But my brother's really late. Do you think I could . . . I could . . ." I stopped talking.

"I suppose your brother has the tickets?" he said.

I nodded mutely, looking down at my feet.

"Sorry," he said. "If you don't have a ticket, you can't come in."

And then he closed the gate and locked it.

There was nothing I could do, really, except stand there getting wetter. That's one problem with having power over fire. My magic tends to be on the spectacular side. I could have had the place on fire in seconds. Spectacular, like I said. But not very practical for this situation.

By halftime, I had been standing outside the Dome for more than an hour. I probably should have left, but I had faith that Peter would show up. My Hawks jacket was soaked, and my new Hawks laces had started to leave green stains on the white canvas parts of my shoes. My glasses kept slipping down my nose, and my braids were sticking to the side of my head. From inside the Dome, I could hear wild cheering from the crowd. Meanwhile, I was outside, getting wet and probably catching a cold.

Finally, I gave up and began trudging toward the bus stop, fighting back the tears.

On my way to the bus stop, a car pulled up to the curve. It was Peter.

"Taranee!" he called from the window. "I'm really, really sorry."

I didn't say anything. I just kept walking.

"Look, the car broke down," he said. "I couldn't help it."

His car looked fine to me. He probably had more trouble trying to tear himself away from Suzanne the supermodel.

Peter jumped out of the car and stood in front of me. I had to stop or try to push him out of the way. Considering that he was much bigger and stronger, stopping was the best option.

"I'll get tickets for next week, I promise!" he cried.

"It's an away game," I replied.

"We'll still go," he said. "We'll make a special trip. Go out to dinner. The works."

I rubbed the rain off my face. "What if the car breaks down . . . again? It seems to be unreliable," I fired back. "Just like some people I know."

"I said I was sorry!" Peter yelled. "My cell phone went dead, so I couldn't call you. I'm really, really sorry."

"Well, go be sorry somewhere else," I said. "I don't want to talk to you." I shouldered past him and continued toward the bus stop.

"Don't be silly, Taranee. You're soaking wet. Get in the car!"

"That wreck? No thanks. I'm waiting for the nice, reliable bus." I prayed that the bus would pull up right then so I wouldn't have to keep having this argument with Peter.

"Taranee, these things happen," he said. He was talking more softly. "I'm sorry it had to be tonight, and I know you're upset. I guess I would be, too. But could you stop being a baby and get in the car? We're both getting wet."

"I'm being a baby?" I cried out. I felt my temper rise. "*I'm* being a baby? Well, at least *I'm* old enough to be on time for things. At least *I'm* old enough to consider other people's feelings and take responsibility. At least *I* didn't go hang out with stupid Suzanne when I had made a promise to my *sister*!"

"Suzanne had nothing to do—" Peter started to say.

"Oh, please," I interrupted. "How stupid do you think I am? Go away. *I don't ever want to see you again!*"

Just then the rain stopped. And for a moment, I felt the world tremble. As the angry words left my mouth, I stared at Peter, aghast.

Guardians should never, ever say such things. *Especially* not in anger.

Irma once transformed a boy when he was acting like a real toad on a date. She ended up turning him into an actual toad!

What I had just said to Peter was way worse than what Irma had done. Why hadn't somebody stopped me? We all *knew* it was dangerous to wish somebody ill. I had told Irma to be careful a zillion times. Yet here I was, telling my own brother I never wanted to see him again.

I looked at Peter. Was he already starting to disappear? Was he getting just the tiniest bit blurry around the edges? No, he was still there, solid as ever. But hurt. I could see it in his eyes.

"Get in the car," he said.

"Peter, I didn't mean—" I tried to explain.

"Then you shouldn't have said it," he snapped. He turned and got into the car.

He was right—even if he didn't know exactly *how* right. I climbed in and we drove in silence for a few blocks. Then Peter reached across and gently punched my shoulder.

"Hey, Miss Hothead," he said. He often called me that when I lost my temper. "Don't look so glum. It's not the end of the world."

"Peter, I'm sorry . . ." I said.

"Yeah, well, so am I," Peter whispered.

The silence was a lot less awkward after that, but I still felt horribly guilty and uneasy.

That night, I had a dream. I was spinning, slowly at first, then faster and faster, as if I were caught in some huge but invisible whirlpool. The unseen currents were pulling at me, drawing me in, and at the center of the whirlpool, something lurked. Something that had been there for ages, listening and waiting. I woke up shivering.

I got out of bed and went to check on Peter. He was in his room listening to music. Nothing out of the ordinary. But I couldn't shake the feeling that when I had said those harsh words to Peter, someone had been *listening*. . . .

2

"How was the game?" asked Will on Saturday morning as we parked our bikes outside the Silver Dragon. It was a sunny day—much different from the previous night's rain and gloom.

"Fine," I muttered. I didn't really want to talk about what had happened. I hadn't talked to Peter yet; the dream had left me feeling too dizzy and weird. When I finally got myself out of bed, Peter had already left to go windsurfing. I could picture him zooming through the waves on his fiberglass board, loving the wind and the speed.

Why hadn't I believed him, when he said the car had broken down? He never lied to me, not about important things. If I had only believed him, I wouldn't have been so furious. And if I hadn't been so furious, I wouldn't have said the horrible things I said.

"Fine?" Will looked skeptical. "That's all I get? No play-by-play account of the exploits of the great what's-his-name . . . Seb Cream?"

"Caine," I said, correcting Will.

"Yeah, him," Will agreed. "You usually go on for hours. Didn't he play after all?"

"Yes." I had seen some of the highlights on the morning's sports report.

"So?" Will urged me to continue.

"So, nothing," I said. I looked around, trying to change the subject. "Hey, isn't that Cornelia?" I pointed to a figure walking toward us.

It was Cornelia, turning up just in time to save me from Will's interrogation. And I needed saving. Will is like a dog with a bone when she's got something on her mind.

"Look what I found," said Cornelia, waving a large library book. "*Magical Mysteries*, by Samuel Goodwise. It's got twelve whole pages on scrying."

That was our project for the weekend. As Guardians go, we were very young, and although we had come a long way, we were still trying to learn more about what we could do. Our magic is not really *like* the kind of magic you read about in books, but we found we could still pick up a few ideas by scouting the library. We had tried to look up *scrying* in the dictionary, but it just said "predicting the future by means of a crystal ball," which sounded like a silly act in a fairground. But according to Samuel Goodwise, it was "using the sight to search out that which is hidden by time, by distance, or by the wiles of humans." Put like that, it seemed like a useful thing to learn.

All five of us—Will, Irma, me, Cornelia, and Hay Lin—went upstairs to Hay Lin's room in her apartment above the Silver Dragon, the restaurant her family runs. Irma crouched over a black baking pan filled with water. Cornelia peered curiously at a pile of potting compost, and Hay Lin had her head out the window, trying to listen to the wind. Will simply watched us with the book open in her lap. Her magic is often the most difficult to figure out, because it's got a bit of everything in it: air, earth, water, *and* fire.

"I don't think this is working," said Cornelia, prodding the dirt with one finger. "All I can tell from this is that it would be great for growing peonies."

"And all *I* can *see* is myself," said Irma. "Mirror, mirror on the wall, who's the cutest of them all? Except this mirror is not really on the wall."

"It says here that scrying takes great skill,

patience, and powers of concentration," said Cornelia, reading over Will's shoulder. "And that vain thirteen-year-old girls checking themselves for pimples hardly ever succeed."

"You're making that up!" cried Irma, snatching her hand away from her nose.

"Only the last part," Cornelia said with a smile.

A thin curl of water rose from Irma's basin, leaped into the air, and hurled itself with great accuracy at Cornelia's nose.

Cornelia ducked. "Watch the book," she hissed. "Miss Pear will be furious!" Miss Pear was the librarian at the Sheffield Institute, where we all went to school.

"True," sighed Irma, and she let the water subside. "But I've been patient for ten whole minutes now, and this scrying stuff still isn't working."

"Maybe we need to be more . . . specific," I said, thinking about it. "Ask a question, and then *really* concentrate."

"Out loud?" Hay Lin let herself slide down from the windowsill.

"Maybe," I said. "I don't know."

"What kind of question?" asked Will.

"Well," I said, "if I'm going to ask a question

of fire, it had better be something that fire knows about."

"Mmmm," said Irma dreamily. "I'm going to ask water what Matt Olsen looks like when he goes swimming with the boys . . . and I bet Will would like a peek, too."

"Irma! Be serious!" Will was blushing furiously. She has a major crush on Matt, but she tries to hide it. Still, it's easy to tell by the way she blushes and walks into door frames every time he passes her in the hallway at school!

I knew what I really wanted to ask, but I wasn't sure whether fire could answer my question. Nevertheless, I closed my eyes and thought about the night before. When I said those awful things to Peter—who or what had heard me?

For a while, nothing happened. I was just about to give up when I felt . . . a twinge. Fire was part of it, and yet it wasn't fire, not really, but something else, something different and twisted. And then it was just like being back in my dream, twisting, spinning, being drawn in. Only this time there was a voice: *Come. Come to me.*

I wanted no part of that sick whirling, and nothing to do with that cold, hungry voice. I fought my way free of it, fought my way back. With a snap that rang loudly inside my head but was probably soundless to my friends, the invisible whirlpool let go of me, and the voice went away. Suddenly there was sunlight, and I was back in Hay Lin's room.

"Did anyone learn anything?" Will said, looking at each of us.

Irma grinned. "Well, I learned that Cornelia never picks her towels up off the floor after she's had a bath."

Cornelia gasped. "You spied on me!"

Irma's grin became even wider. "Actually, that was just a lucky guess. But I did find the ring my mom lost last week. Although how we're going to get hold of it is another matter. It's stuck in the bathroom drain."

"Anyone else?" Will asked.

Cornelia shook her head, still looking annoyed.

Hay Lin bit her lip, skeptical of the whole exercise. "I'm not sure," she said. "It's not very clear."

"Try again, then," suggested Will.

I got up abruptly. "Not me," I said. "You try if you want to, but I've had enough for one day."

"Taranee," said Will, looking at me more closely. "Are you okay? You look . . . well, you don't look good."

I didn't feel good. I felt queasy. And frightened. And chilled to the bone. But I couldn't say exactly why.

"I'm fine," I muttered.

"Enough work," said Irma decisively, putting her arm around me. "What this girl needs is a snack and a few laughs. Anyone know a good joke?"

🜨 🜨 🜨 🜨 🜨

Some food and a few of Irma's silly stories eased the tension in my stomach. Hay Lin's parents let us all eat lunch at a table in the restaurant. But just as I was taking a last bite with my chopsticks, I saw my father come through the door of the Silver Dragon. The expression on his face made me sick to my stomach all over again.

"Taranee," he said in a very serious tone. "Peter is . . . well, he didn't come back this morning from the beach with the others. He'll probably call us soon from . . . from some other part of the beach, but . . . your mother and I think you should come home now."

I looked at my friends in a panic. Then I quickly gathered my things to follow my dad home.

3

It was awful. I felt so ill I could hardly think. I heard my mother talking to an endless line of people in uniforms. Her voice was sharper than steel, and she kept at them, asking question after question. My mother is a judge, so she is used to dealing with the police, but her fear about Peter made her completely ruthless.

Three words kept ringing in my ears like the echoes of a huge gong: lost at sea.

Friends said, *He's such a strong swimmer.* Family said, *Maybe there's no phone where he came ashore.* I supposed that Peter could have been in a burger joint somewhere, completely unaware that we were worried. I wanted to believe that. But the sick feeling in my stomach wouldn't let up.

"The Coast Guard is looking," one police

officer said. "They're very good at their job."

"They have a chopper up," another one said. "No doubt they'll find him soon."

No one said *drowned*. No one said *lost*. And no one said, *It's all your fault, Taranee*.

But it was. I just knew it. My ill wish had come true.

⚬ ⚬ ⚬ ⚬ ⚬

I let myself out of the house as quietly as I could. My friends would still be at Hay Lin's, and I needed their help. This was not something I could do on my own. I had left my parents a note— *Gone to find Peter*, it said—because I didn't think they would let me leave without a good excuse. I really hoped I—and Peter—would be back before they found the note. I couldn't risk Hay Lin's parents spotting me and calling my parents, so I stood in the street just outside the restaurant. Another perk of being a Guardian is that I have telepathic powers. I just had to look up at Hay Lin's window and think really hard that I wanted one of them to see me. Will opened the window and spotted me almost instantly.

We'll be right down, she said telepathically.

"Have they found him?" asked Hay Lin, coming out of the Silver Dragon's back door a few moments later.

I shook my head. They all stood there, looking awkward. I suppose I would have, too, if I had been one of them. Finally, Irma put her arm around me.

"It was all my fault," I said.

"Don't be silly," said Cornelia. "How could it be?"

I told them exactly how it could be my fault.

They all looked shaken.

"But I say awful things all the time," said Irma. "Especially to my little brother. How can I avoid it? How can anyone avoid it, if they've got an annoying brother?"

"Maybe it's not because of what you said," said Cornelia. "Maybe it's just a coincidence."

I shook my head. "It *is* because of what I said. I know it. You've got to help me. We've got to *find* him."

"I don't know," said Cornelia. "I mean, the scrying thing wasn't going too well. Maybe it's not something we can do."

"Of course it is," Will said. Then she turned to face me. "There's no question. We have to do something to help Peter."

I gave Will a thankful smile.

"Irma," Will said, "you were better than any of us at scrying. What should we do?"

"Hmmm," she said thoughtfully. "I'm going to need more water. And I know just where to go!"

Irma took us to a place with a huge garden that she said had a pond. The fence around the garden looked very unfriendly—clearly it was meant to keep visitors out. The sharp black points on the top jutted up toward the sky like spears.

"Do we have to go in there?" asked Hay Lin, eyeing the ivy-infested jungle beyond the fence. "It's probably crawling with bugs and spiders and things."

"Couldn't we just use the pool at my house?" said Cornelia. "It's a lot cleaner."

"It's chlorinated," said Irma, as if that explained everything. "And your pest of a little sister would interrupt us every five minutes. Besides, no Guardian I ever heard of scried in a condo swimming pool. We need a little atmosphere. Here, boost me up."

"I heard the man who lives here is kinda weird," said Hay Lin, looking up at the fence.

"Who? Mr. Buckingham?" Irma asked. "I think that's just a rumor. But he does have a few a few big dogs."

"Big dogs?" I said, hearing my voice go thin.

"A couple of Dobermans," Irma explained.

"But I'm sure they won't bother us. Come on, let's do this while we're still young and cute."

I didn't want to. I didn't like spiders, and I wasn't in the habit of breaking in to other people's gardens. I didn't much like dogs, either, especially when they were big, dark, and fierce. But I wanted my brother back. And if this was what it took, then . . .

I climbed the fence.

🥚🥚🔺◎🥚

The pond that Irma was talking about was more like a large lake. In the middle was an island, crowded with huge, dark, rhododendron bushes.

"Here's the best place," whispered Irma.

"Why are you whispering?" whispered Cornelia. "I thought you said he was deaf?"

"He is," said Irma, without raising her voice.

We crossed a small Japanese-style stone bridge that led to the island. Much of the large pond was choked with weeds and fallen leaves, but here, in the dense shadow of the rhododendron, the water was black and mirror-still. I could see what Irma meant by atmosphere. This place certainly had plenty—any moment now, a flock of bats would probably come flapping out of the mouth of some hidden cave.

"All right," said Irma, facing the water.

"Let's see what we can do now that we're here."

She closed her eyes for a moment, concentrating. At her feet, the water began to swirl in strange patterns, then abruptly became still. We all stared at the surface. There was a glimpse of sky—not the gray one above us, but a bluer one, filled with seagulls. Then the image faded, and there was only still, black water once more.

We all looked at Irma. She shook her head.

"He was on water," Irma said, "but he isn't now. He's gone beyond water."

Did that mean ashore? I hoped so. But where?

"Let me try," said Hay Lin.

She raised her hands, and suddenly a stiff cold wind swept over us, a wind with a sea smell to it, and a spray of water, fine as mist. For a moment I could hear surf, and screaming gulls.

"He was in the wind," said Hay Lin, and hesitated. "I know this sounds spooky, but he's gone beyond air, too."

Beyond *air*? How could you go beyond air?

"I'll try," Cornelia said.

"Please," I said. "Maybe he is . . . underground, in a cave or something, and that's why water and air can't reach him."

When it comes to trying something new and

strange, Cornelia is often skeptical. But when she saw my tears, her face softened.

She went down on one knee and put her hand on the dark, loamy soil.

The island *trembled*. The glossy, dark rhododendron leaves shook, and a couple of startled pigeons took off and flew away. Cornelia raised her hand, and the ground stopped trembling.

I looked at her. We all did.

"Well?" I finally said.

She just shook her head, her jaw set.

The lump in the pit of my stomach grew.

"You're going to tell me that he was on earth but has gone beyond it," I finally whispered.

"I don't say things like that," she muttered. But it was what she had seen.

I sat down abruptly on the edge of the bridge.

"Taranee . . ." Will said gently.

I looked at her, or tried to. My glasses had misted over, and everything was blurry.

"I . . . I'm not sure how good I am at this, but I tried to ask a question, too. I asked if Peter were beyond life—and I don't think he is."

"How can he be alive, and still be beyond . . . beyond . . ." I couldn't finish the sentence.

"I don't know," said Will. "But if we all ask at the same time, maybe we can find out where to start looking." She called the Heart of Candracar.

The Heart is always with Will, but not always visible. Usually, it appears as a clear, round crystal held in a clasp of silvery metal. But just then, the crystal had already begun to leak light—a glint of green, a glint of blue, and then a glint of warm pink. The crystal is not just the Heart of Candracar, it is the heart of all of us. And seeing it, feeling it, made me . . . different. I've always loved the story of the Phoenix, the golden bird that is reborn in fire and rises from its own ashes. That's how the Heart made me feel: like I was being given new life, and a new fire. The hopelessness dropped away from me like flakes of papery ash.

One by one, the Heart drew us in, until we were all clasping it—five hands, one on top of the other.

"Think hard," said Will. "And ask this question: Where did Peter go?"

It was the perfect question. And when we all thought about the question together, it made our power much stronger. What we do together is always much stronger than what we do apart.

The earth moved, like a huge animal rippling the skin on its back. The winds whirled around us, whipping up leaves and dirt and pond water, so that we felt as if we were standing in the eye of a small hurricane. All around us, water rose like a huge, dark green wall. Inside the wall, a picture was forming.

"Wind shaped this place," said Hay Lin.

"And water," said Irma.

"And rock," said Cornelia.

I didn't say anything. Again, I had felt that hint of fire that was not . . . not quite fire.

The picture was clear now, as clear as if we were staring at a movie projection screen. There was an island, not very large, and mostly all rock. From a wind-and-wave-carved narrow base, two humps rose, with a jagged cleft in the middle, making the rock look like a cracked heart. Seagulls circled, riding the breeze. Behind the rock, the sun had slowly begun to set.

"Anyone know this place?" asked Will.

Hay Lin nodded. "It's up near Pleasance. Just off the coast there. I remember it because . . . well, once you've seen it, you don't forget it."

Will sighed and opened her hand, releasing the crystal. The wind dropped; the earth came to rest; the water settled neatly back into its pond, and my fire died.

"Has it got a name?" she asked.

Hay Lin shrugged. "You don't forget that, either," she said. "It's called Heartbreak Island."

4

Pleasance wasn't too far from Heatherfield, so we quickly caught a bus there. Once we arrived in the town, we pooled our money and rented a boat for the ride to Heartbreak Island. The boat was tiny, but with one of us holding power over air, and another over the water, that hardly mattered. Hay Lin and Irma worked their magic. Immediately, the nylon sail bulged, and with the waves nudging us along at Irma's bidding, it was like riding a speedboat.

Heavy, dark clouds hung above us, turning the sea nearly black. It was cold out, and I shivered, wishing I had brought a sweater.

"There it is," said Hay Lin, pointing.

And there was Heartbreak Island. The island looked black against the sunset, a knobby hump that jutted out of the water.

"It looks . . . out of place, somehow," I said, hesitantly. "Like it shouldn't even be here."

"Three hundred years ago, it wasn't," said Hay Lin. "One day, a couple of centuries ago, a fisherman nearly ran his boat into an island that had never been there before. Scientists say it was volcanic activity, but people in Pleasance have a lot of stories about this place."

"Is there a beach somewhere?" asked Irma, watching the way the waves broke against the rocks.

"Maybe Cornelia can make us one," Hay Lin said.

Cornelia didn't answer. She was busy clutching the side of the boat. Being an earth girl, she much preferred being on land to being in the water.

"Let's go around the island," I said, "and look."

My eyes were already skimming across the rocks, searching. Was there anything, any sign, that Peter was here or had been here? Maybe Cornelia was right. Maybe we really weren't good at scrying.

"There *is* a beach," said Hay Lin, pointing. "Is that where we want to go?"

"Let's go in," I said. "I think I see something . . ."

Irma calmed the breaking waves, and Hay Lin turned the wind to guide the boat in among the rocky spurs. Suddenly Cornelia let out a yell.

"Reef!" she screamed. "Watch out!"

"Where?" Hay Lin asked.

"Below us!" Cornelia cried. "Lift the boat. Irma, *lift the boat!*"

I could see it too, something dark and sharp in the water below us. Irma gestured frantically, and the boat rose like a bobbing cork on the back of a huge and sudden wave. There was a scraping sound as the reef scored the hull, and then we shot through the narrow opening, much too fast. The boat jerked, bucked, and flipped onto its side. We all spilled out and then I was splashing and crying out, tumbling and coughing because I had gasped in a mouthful of water.

I don't want to drown, I thought. Then I realized I wasn't going to. Not in water that was only a foot deep . . .

I stood up carefully, rearranging my glasses. The others were standing up too, shaken but unhurt. Even the boat was undamaged except for a couple of scrapes on the fiberglass hull, as if a very large cat had scratched it.

I waded onto the beach, heading for the shape I had seen, lying in the water. It gleamed in the gathering dusk, with blue and yellow stripes along its length. It was Peter's Windsurfer. Or rather, one jagged, broken end of the board.

🝐 🝐 🝐 🝐 🝐

We searched the island for Peter by climbing all the way around it, across tumbled boulders and up slippery rock slopes. We called out Peter's name until our voices were hoarse. Eventually, we came back to the beach, wet, cold, and exhausted, having found absolutely nothing.

"It's too dark now," said Hay Lin. "We could walk right past him and never see him. And with all the cliffs and the cracks in the ground around here, one of us might end up breaking an ankle. Or worse."

I could hear her teeth chattering. "Let's build a fire," I said. "There's no reason to freeze."

There wasn't much to build a fire with. There were no trees on the island, only rocks and weeds. But starting fires out of nothing was something I could do. We gathered a pile of weeds and rocks, and I called on my magic to light it. We might still be tired and hungry, I thought. But at least I would see to it that we were warm.

Cornelia had a bar of chocolate in the pocket of her jacket. It was somewhat wet, of course, and there was only one small square for each of us, but it was a lot better than nothing.

"Thanks," I said, taking a small square.

She just nodded. She sat on a rock with her legs curled to one side, mermaid-style. The rest of us were a bedraggled-looking lot, but she managed to look as if her windblown hair was *meant* to be that way, as if some stylist had just this minute arranged each silky blond hair for a fashion shoot. It's called style. I wish I had more of it.

I stared into the fire. Peter's Windsurfer was there, but Peter wasn't. Where could he have gone from there, except back into the sea? Only, Irma had said he wasn't in water. And Will had said he was not beyond life. I clung to that.

"Taranee!" Hay Lin called. "Look!"

I pushed my glasses up on my nose. And then I saw what Hay Lin was pointing at.

A vague, greenish glow, eerie and almost fluorescent, could be seen off in the distance. And it seemed to be coming from *within* the island.

"What is *that*?" I said.

"Looks like somebody forgot to close the fridge," said Irma. "A very *big* fridge."

"The light in our fridge isn't *green*," Hay Lin said.

"Well, that light is," said Will. "And I think we'd better find out where it's coming from."

"I'm not sure I like this," said Irma, for once looking serious and somewhat subdued. "There is something not right about that glow."

But Will was already off, and whatever was making that light, I felt, had to have something to do with Peter. So I followed. Hay Lin drifted up the rock face alongside me, as effortlessly as if she weighed nothing at all. She's the only one of us who can fly. That's what having power over air will do.

"It's deep," called Will from above. "I think it could be the opening to some kind of cave."

I tried to climb faster, feeling both tense and excited. Maybe Peter *was* underground, as I had first thought.

Oh, please, I thought, let him be all right.

"We've got to find some way of getting down there," Will said. "And it would be nice if we could do it without breaking any bones. It drops sharply, and I don't see an end to it."

"We could tie ourselves together," Hay Lin said. "And I could sort of . . . ask air to hold us up."

"Can you do that?" I asked. "For all four of us?"

"I think so," Hay Lin said. "Or we could do it two at a time, that might be safer."

"We don't have a rope," said Will.

Hay Lin smiled. "Maybe not. But I'm not exactly short of cords . . ."

That was true. Whatever Hay Lin wore, there were always at least three or four brightly colored cords or laces involved.

"It's simpler if I do it," said Cornelia, and raised her hands.

There was a rumble and a clatter of falling rock as earth began to rearrange itself.

"Watch out!" I cried. "Peter could be down there!"

Cornelia immediately stopped.

"Sorry," she said. "I didn't think of that." She peered into the crack. "It's not quite finished," she added, "but we can use it if we're careful."

Thick dust flew up in the green glow. It took a moment before the air settled enough for me to see what Cornelia had done.

She had probably, before I interrupted her, meant to make a staircase, but what we had now was a row of rough, rocky bumps, like spikes on a dragon's back. And she was right. They could be used, if we were careful.

"Well," said Will. "I don't suppose there's any point in waiting. Let's go."

Slowly, we began to descend.

"I feel like the filling in a sandwich," muttered Irma from in between the rocks just behind me. "A sandwich made with very hard bread!"

In places, the narrow seam dropped almost straight down, so that my fingers hurt from clinging to the rough bumps of Cornelia's ladder. Elsewhere, it leveled out but became narrower, so that we had to crawl on hands and knees, and even on our bellies.

"How much longer?" I gasped at Will, who was in front of me.

"Can't see," she muttered back.

It felt as if we had been crawling and scrabbling in the eerie green not-quite-darkness for half the night. Could seams like this one go down below sea level without being flooded?

What if water suddenly came rushing up through the crack? Would we be able to escape?

You're not going to drown, I told myself. You have Irma right here. And no, the tunnel isn't really narrowing around you, and yes, there really is enough air to breathe, even if it smells funny.

Suddenly, I bumped into Will. She had stopped abruptly just in front of me.

"Look," she whispered. "I think we're here."

I moved up next to her on my hands and knees. A little further ahead, the tunnel widened sharply, and there were steps carved into the rock, steps that did not look at all like Cornelia's unfinished dragon spikes.

Carefully, we edged forward. Will had one hand curled around the Heart of Candracar. I didn't know if it was just for general comfort, or so she would be ready if we were attacked.

The steps ended in a large, cavernous chamber. And although there was no one there, the chamber did not feel empty. There was *something* there. In a wide, strangely carved stone basin, something swirled and flickered, glowing sullenly with a thick, phosphorous light. A whirlpool, like the one in my dream. A maelstrom. But whatever it was, it was nothing as simple as water.

The floor of the chamber was covered with fine sand. And there, scrawled in a casual hand, was a message.

Enter, Guardians—if you dare.

Placed neatly next to the message was Peter's watch.

5

I gently picked up the watch. It was the one that our parents had just given Peter for his birthday.

"Is it Peter's?" Will asked tentatively.

I nodded, unable to speak.

"Then someone brought him here," Will said. We all stared at the maelstrom.

"Irma . . ." I said. But she just shook her head, shuddering.

"I'm not touching that," she said. "It doesn't want me to. It doesn't listen to me." Irma paused. "It isn't really water."

I went down on one knee by the maelstrom's edge and inserted a cautious fingertip. With a yelp, I snatched my finger back.

"Well, it's not fire, either," I said. "It's burning me! Fire wouldn't."

Will surveyed the scene. "It's both," she

said. "Waterfire. Water and fire combined."

We all stared at each other. Water and fire don't combine. Ever. They can't.

Except here the elements had.

"And just how are we supposed to get through *that*?" whispered Irma.

I didn't know. But whoever had written that message seemed to think there *was* a way.

"Let's ask the Heart," said Will quietly, and she brought it into her hand. Together, we clasped it, letting its gentle white glow wash over us.

"Heart of Candracar," said Will, with great concentration. "Show us the way."

I had said that fire and water never combine, but in the Heart of Candracar, they meet. The Heart of Candracar holds us all together, and has room enough for all of our personalities. Irma and I are very different from each other. But when we both hold the Heart, we are closer than sisters. It's the magic of friendship.

I closed my eyes and knew that what I then saw the others saw, too. A huge pillared hall, so vast its walls seemed to recede into infinity. A light, just like the Heart's own glow. And at its center, a presence, gentle but strong.

"Welcome, Guardians."

It was the voice of the Oracle. I can't explain

how, but I *knew* that even though we were still standing on the sandy floor of the rock chamber deep inside Heartbreak Island, we were also in the Temple of Candracar. And though I spoke, explaining about my angry words and Peter's disappearance, I had the feeling that I didn't really need to say any of it; the Oracle already knew.

"It was my fault," I said miserably. "I shouldn't have wished him ill."

"A wish is indeed a strong force," the Oracle decreed. "Especially a Guardian's wish."

I hung my head, feeling horribly guilty. But the Oracle smiled, and my guilt was eased.

"Have courage," the Oracle said. "Your words were unwise, but there was no deep malice in them. Did you truly wish to harm your brother?"

"No!" I said, a little too forcefully.

"Much greater faults go unpunished every day." The Oracle's calm voice continued. "Your mistake has brought you to this challenge, and you must believe there is a reason for that. Without mistakes, there would be no learning, and from your small stumble, a greater good may come, and an ancient wrongness may be put right."

"But the maelstrom . . . we're stuck," I said. "We don't know how to cross it. We don't know what it *is*."

There was a sigh. Then the Oracle spoke again.

"I must tell you a story," the Oracle began. "Once, long ago, there was a young woman, not much older than you. She had a touch of magic, and she used it in little ways, to sway men and women to her will. One day she saw a young man and wanted him to love her; but the young man was stubborn in his devotion to another. And so the sorceress sought to make that other girl disappear. She nearly succeeded, by calling upon many mean spirits from the worlds beyond. The Guardians at that time defeated the evil she had called up, but in the confusion, the young sorceress found a terrible means of escape. Her magic unlocked a stronger one. She disappeared, spinning in a vortex of unnatural magic, a great whirling current that sucked her in so that she was beyond the reach of the Guardians."

My eyes snapped open involuntarily, and I stared at the maelstrom.

"This? This is the vortex?" I asked.

"Yes," the Oracle said. "The Guardians dared not go near the whirling chaos. All they could do was raise this island to hide the vortex."

"What happened to the sorceress?" Hay Lin asked.

"I do not know," the Oracle said.

That startled all of us. We had become convinced over time that the Oracle knew everything.

"How . . . how come?" Irma asked.

The Oracle held up his hands. Between them spun a twisted hoop, almost a figure eight.

"Do you know what this is?" he asked.

"It's a Möbius strip," I said. "It's a sort of . . . two-dimensional infinity."

"And now?" the Oracle asked as he changed the figure. It became a true figure eight. The Oracle manipulated the figure again slightly, so that one of the circles was much smaller than the other.

"It's . . . an ordinary figure of eight," I said.

"And what has happened to infinity?" he challenged.

"I . . . I don't understand," I confessed.

"The sorceress found a way to twist nature," the Oracle explained. "She twisted it so violently that she warped a little bit of time and space into a tiny, separate loop. I see the greater circle of infinity—but into her small, twisted circle, I cannot go. Yet I think you can, because she wants you to. Have you not heard her calling?"

I remembered the cold, hungry voice.

"You mean we should just let that thing . . .

suck us in?" Irma said, sounding revolted.

"I think you will do what you must," the Oracle responded calmly. "Trust your heart."

The Oracle's presence faded.

"It's so cold it burns. . . ." I whispered. I was still trying to process what this element before us was and how to control it.

"It feels so unnatural," said Cornelia shakily.

How had Peter gone through the vortex? He must have. There was nowhere else he could have gone. And this clearly illustrated the way anyone could go beyond water, beyond earth, and beyond air—and still not be beyond life.

"Maybe the Heart will shield us," said Will.

"I could go alone," I said. "Peter is my brother."

"No way," said Irma firmly. "The maelstrom wants a Guardian. But I say, let's give it just a little bit more than she bargained for. Not one Guardian, but five."

Irma stretched and then started to transform herself. Will immediately did the same, and the rest of us followed. Soon, in that cavern, there were no longer five tired girls in jeans and sneakers. When we're Guardians, we are something else. It's not just the wings, or the clothes, though both look good. Cornelia, of course, looks elegantly perfect, as always. The funny thing is, the rest of us look perfect, too. Not alike, not at all. Hay Lin looks perfectly Hay Lin. Will is even more perfectly Will. I guess even I look perfect, in a Taranee sort of way. It *feels* totally different, too. It's like a sleek, wildcat sensation of being able to do just about anything. This is what I meant when I said that being a Guardian of the Veil is *fun*. Sometimes it is so much fun I forget that I'm meant to be saving the world.

Only this time it wasn't the world we were here to save. It was my brother, Peter.

"If we're doing this," I said, "Let's do it now."

We stepped on to the rim of the basin, hands clasped together.

Irma eyed the surly green not-quite-water. "I usually like my baths hotter than this," she joked. "Oh, well."

"Heart of Candracar, shield us," said Will.

And then we jumped.

6

As we entered the passageway, I felt a pressure so fierce I couldn't breathe. Hay Lin's hand was wrenched from my grasp; for a few desperate seconds I clung to Will, but then she, too, was torn from me. I whirled and spun through nothingness. Then something hit me hard, and for a few moments, everything went dark. It took a while before I could finally catch my breath.

"What happened?" muttered Hay Lin in a dazed voice.

I opened my eyes. We hadn't jumped at all. We were back where we had started. Or at least, that was what it looked like when I finally sat up and took in my surroundings.

We were in a cavernous, underground chamber that looked like a carved stone basin with a sandy floor. The sullen green of the maelstrom gave the chamber a weird, eerie glow.

Irma had climbed halfway to her feet and was looking around her with the same dazed expression that was probably on my face.

"But we were just . . . we just came . . ." She stared at the basin and the green pool.

Will looked as if she were out cold. I touched her face. Her skin was chilled and clammy.

"Is she okay?" asked Hay Lin.

"I don't know," I said.

"Where are we?" Irma asked. "Have we . . . moved at all?"

"Of course we have," said Cornelia in a voice that suggested that Irma's question was silly. "The stairs are on the other side of the chamber, here."

She was right. And what was more—the maelstrom in the basin here swirled counterclockwise, not clockwise as before. The chamber was a mirror image of the one we'd just left.

Will began to stir. Irma helped her sit up.

"We're here," Irma said. "Wherever *here* is."

"Oh," said Will, weakly. "It looks a lot like . . . like where we were before."

And then a choking noise escaped her.

"Will?" I said, rushing over to grab her hand. "What's wrong?"

Will didn't speak. And then Hay Lin pointed

to the Heart, which had spilled onto the ground from Will's shivering hand.

"Look!" Hay Lin explained.

The Heart of Candracar was no longer a perfect sphere of clear and pulsing light. At its core, a murky, green-tinged twist had appeared, like a crack in a porcelain plate.

"Look," whispered Hay Lin once more. "The Heart is broken."

We all stood there looking at it, completely stunned, except for Will, who sat in the sand, shaking uncontrollably. How could the Heart be broken?

"It's just a crack," said Irma hopefully. "It's not as if it's really, *really* broken."

"Not really, *really* broken?" mimicked Cornelia. "Why, thank you for that brilliant analysis, Ms. Lair."

"Cornelia," muttered Irma. "Just because you always know—"

"Be quiet, both of you," I said. "There's something wrong with Will."

It was hard to tell in the horrid green glow that made everyone look sick, but Will's face looked even paler than ours did.

"Will?" I touched her forehead gently. It was damp with sweat.

She opened her eyes, then quickly shut them.

"Will, how do you feel?" I asked.

"Dizzy," she muttered. "Taranee, it *hurts*."

"Where?" I asked.

"Everywhere," she said, shakily. "Inside."

"Can you stand?" I asked her.

"Think so," she said. "I'll try."

Cornelia and I helped her to sit up against the edge of the maelstrom basin. Hay Lin picked up the damaged Heart and put it into Will's trembling hands. Will's eyes filled with tears.

"I was supposed to look after it," she moaned.

"It's not your fault," I said, stroking her arm. "And it's not . . ." I hesitated, thinking of Irma's statement that the Heart wasn't really, *really* broken. ". . . It's not shattered or anything. Maybe we can find a way to mend it."

"Sure," muttered Cornelia under her breath.

I glared at her. "It's a magical object. Maybe magic can heal it."

"We'll ask the Oracle," Hay Lin said. "When we get . . . when we get back. Right now we still have to find Taranee's brother."

"I think Will should stay here," said Irma. "She's not fit to go anywhere. And maybe one of us should stay with her."

But Will shook her head.

"No," she said. "Together. We have to stay together." And she put her hands on the side of the basin and pulled herself up to stand, hunched and shivering, on her own two feet.

"Are you sure?" I said.

She nodded again. "Positive."

"All right, then. Let's go," I said and turned, heading for the steps.

"Just like fire," said Cornelia, in a slightly disgusted tone.

I spun around. "What?" I demanded.

"What you're doing right now," Cornelia said. "Charging off without bothering to make a plan."

"How *can* we make a plan?" I asked. "We don't know the first thing about this place."

"Fine. Have it your way," Cornelia snapped.

I had had just about enough of Miss Cornelia.

"Peter's my brother, and I'm going to look for him," I said, and continued up the steps without waiting for a reply. It was no time to argue.

"Wait," said Irma, scrambling to follow. "I'll come with you."

A few minutes later Cornelia and Hay Lin took hold of Will and followed us up the steps.

�’ ꮛ ⬟ ◉ ꮛ

The steps were much wider than they had been on Heartbreak Island. They were smooth and shiny with wear. And this was a real tunnel, not a rough crack one could barely slip through. Here, one could walk upright all the way to the surface.

Soon, I could see a pale light at the end of the tunnel. I slowed down, and ended up creeping forward on my hands and knees. I kept thinking of the cold, hungry voice. We were there because someone wanted us there. Someone who had written us a message in the sand—*Enter . . . if you dare*. It seemed a good idea to assume there might be a welcome committee, and that it might not be the kind of welcome we would want to walk into unwarned.

To my surprise, there was no one there—at least, no one in the immediate vicinity. The barren rocks of the island were deserted. But away from the rocks, it looked as though we were coming in to the middle of a city—of some sort.

The sea all around us was covered with rafts and rigs and gangways, with houseboats and gondolas and barges and every other kind of floating craft imaginable, and quite a few I was pretty certain no one had ever imagined. Many of the rafts were connected by elaborate bridges. Above it all, the sky was dark and empty. No moon, no stars. It made me shiver to look at it, so alien and empty. I quickly lowered my eyes.

The light I had seen came from the sea. A pale light filtered up from the depths that made everything I saw look not quite real. Yet there were clearly real people down there, even if none of them happened to be human. Most of the inhabitants reminded me of frogs. Out of water, they waddled with flippered legs, and they had smooth, hairless skins that were speckled in various greenish shades. Few of them bothered with the bridges to cross the water. To get from one raft to another, they simply slipped into the water with amphibious ease. The sea was crowded with them, as were the rafts and platforms.

"They look like frogs!" whispered Irma. "Very big frogs . . ."

I nodded. They were very nearly human-sized, most of them. They didn't seem sinister or dangerous. But every once in a while, they would scatter and make way for something much more predatory-looking: fanged and scaled reptiles with razor-sharp spines along their backs. If most of the city's inhabitants looked like frogs, these looked like giant Gila monsters.

"I think it's the scaly ones we have to worry about," I whispered back. "They seem . . . mean. And the minute they catch sight of us, they'll know we're strangers."

Irma snorted. "I think I can convince those creatures that we look just like them."

"Mmmm," said Will. "But can you also let us all breathe below the surface, if we have to?"

Irma looked thoughtful for moment. "I think so," she said.

"She *thinks* so," said Cornelia. "Well, good. Let's all hurry up and trust her with our lives."

"Why are you acting like this?" I asked her. Cornelia's attitude was not helping the situation at all. I looked closely at her. What was going on?

"Like what?" she asked, all innocent.

"Snide. Sarcastic," I explained.

"Well, *excuse* me," said Cornelia. "I'm just trying to be the voice of reason around here."

"Well, who hired *you* for the job?" I asked, losing my patience.

"Could you keep your voices down?" said Hay Lin. "Unless you really want those fanged creatures down there to hear us?"

Angry looks were exchanged. Even Hay Lin, who was usually always so cheerful, looked irritated.

"I'm going down there," I said, "if Irma will help. Maybe someone knows where Peter is."

"I'll help," said Irma loyally. "It's nice to know *somebody* trusts me."

"Well, someone should stay here and guard the chamber," Cornelia said. "Any survivors need to have at least a tiny chance of making it back to Heatherfield."

"Are you volunteering?" I asked.

"I guess so," she said. I couldn't help noticing that Cornelia looked a little hurt.

I felt a pang of guilt. Usually, we wouldn't have split up like that. But just then, with her in her present mood, I really didn't want Cornelia around. It made me upset to feel that way. In any event, it did make sense to guard the chamber.

"I'll stay, too," said Hay Lin. "Just in case."

"You don't have to," Cornelia said. "But I would like . . . I mean, it's more *sensible* not to be alone."

Will looked unhappy. "We should stay together," she said. "We're better that way."

Not right now, I thought, not the way we keep arguing and fighting over everything.

"You still look pale," I said. "You should stay with Cornelia and Hay Lin for now."

She shook her head. "I have a feeling . . . I need to come. And I'm feeling much better now."

She didn't look better. But of all the Guardians, Will was my best friend, and I was glad to have her come with me.

7

The city was making me seasick as we traveled to find some answers. Nothing was on solid ground; everything bobbed and wobbled, moving with our movements and the ripples of the sea. And although there were lamps and lanterns on most of the rafts and bridges, most of the lights were coming from the sea. The light did not come just from the reflections on the surface but from down in the deep, where the sea glowed like a lit swimming pool at night.

Irma was peering into the water, looking absolutely fascinated.

"It goes down for *miles*," she said in awe.

I wasn't sure about actual miles, but it was quite clear that this city was like an iceberg: nine-tenths of it was below the surface. The city didn't have tall buildings—it had deep ones.

The illusion Irma provided seemed to be working—no one appeared to pay much attention to us. All around us, frog people were moving in a steady stream, some in a hurried and businesslike manner, others waddling or swimming in a more leisurely way.

Suddenly there was a disturbance in the water. Splashes and high-pitched cries were followed by something that sounded almost like a snarling laugh. Then there came a bellow and another splash, and out of the water, closely followed by a pair of particularly ugly reptiles, lunged a sleek, green-speckled body. It landed on the dock by our feet with a wet slap. I stepped back involuntarily, slipped, and fell almost on top of the froggish body in front of me.

"Eeeeek!" the creature yelled, rolling out of the way. Then he shot to his feet for a quick getaway. He almost made it, too. But I had slowed him down just a little, and before he had time to slip into a narrow vent at the back of one of the raft-houses, a scaled claw seized him by the scruff of the neck. There was a wail of terror from the frog boy, and then a thin shriek of pain as one of the reptiles casually pushed him against the wall and held him pinned there with a spiked foot.

All the other frog people on the raft froze in the middle of whatever they were doing. Then there was a general slither, and within minutes, the crowd had simply melted away, into buildings or into the water, so that the poor frog boy, who was no bigger than an eight-year-old human child, was alone with his captors. And us.

The biggest of the reptiles yawned widely, exposing fangs that would have made a crocodile envious, and the frog boy's skin turned from olive to pasty white.

Then the reptile drew back its hand for a blow.

"Stop!" I yelled. Drawing their attention might not have been the smartest thing in the world, but how could I just stand there and let them do . . . do whatever they were going to do to such a small and helpless victim? "Let him go!"

The smaller reptile still held the struggling frog boy pinned against the wall. The other slowly turned and looked at me. Those pale yellow eyes, that fanged grin—the last time I had met something that looked like that, it was in a nightmare.

"Thssssiiieff," it hissed. It raised one claw to lift a fold of the fishnet-like toga it was wearing and flashed a badge of some kind at me—a crown, it looked like, gold on green. Then it turned its back on me, as if that were explanation enough, and once more raised its hand.

Oh, no, you don't, I thought. And I set fire to its toga.

For a moment, it simply stared at the flames with a puzzled look on its scaly face. Then it roared in terror, and started batting at the fire with both stubby arms. It could have dived overboard in seconds, but that simple solution didn't seem to occur to it.

The smaller reptile looked just as stunned as the other at first, then let go of the frog boy and retreated from the fire. The frog boy immediately slipped to one side, grabbed me by the arm, and dived for the vent he had been making for in the first place, dragging me along with him. I was so surprised I didn't even try to resist. The grate blocking the vent swung to the side at his touch, and in we went, head first, frog boy, then me. Irma and Will, who had gotten a last-minute grip on my left ankle, followed. We tumbled a great distance before ending up in a pile at the bottom of a sort of tube.

I think it was an airshaft. From where we sat, other tubes led off in three different directions, all sloping downward. The only way up was the slippery pipe through which we had just fallen. Climbing it looked like a near-impossible task. In any case, there were probably two very angry reptiles waiting for us at the top.

"Great," muttered Irma. "And how do we get out of *this*?" She glared at the frog boy, who now squatted a few feet away, eyeing us with what looked like wide-eyed amazement. I couldn't be sure, though—maybe his eyes always bulged like that.

Warily he inched a little closer, then reached out and cautiously touched my hand. His webbed fingers were wet, but soft and smooth.

"You are! Oh, yes!" he said, "You really are!"

"What?" I asked. I wondered what he saw.

"Queen people! And you made Truefire! Wait till the queen hears of this, no peace in Stromtown then, for certain sure, no, none at all, oh, no!"

Queen people? Whatever he meant by that, he could clearly tell we weren't town folk. I looked at Irma.

"I thought you were dealing with the disguise thing," I whispered to Irma.

She looked faintly embarrassed. "I was. But what with all the excitement . . . well, I guess my control slipped a little."

I turned to the frog boy. "Who is this queen you're talking about?" Could she be some descendant of the sorceress? I wondered.

He looked shocked. "Who is the queen?" he repeated. "Who is the *queen*? Oh, bad trouble, bad trouble. Queen people don't know the queen. Just wait. Just wait till she hears. Oh, no. Queen people will be just bones in the water, clean bones, oh, yes."

He was beginning to get on my nerves. "Are you planning to turn us in?" I asked him. "I saved your life. Are you going to pay me back by telling on me to this queen of yours?"

Nervously he clutched at the bruise on his chest where the big bully had pushed him.

"Reb won't harm, oh, no, not harm who helped him," the frog boy said. "But the queen knows. Queen knows everything, oh, yes. She has the Spinies. They hurt me. Will hurt you. She has the Merefire. She *knows*, oh, yes! And she collects queen people."

Collects? That . . . didn't sound good. It made me think of carefully preserved butterflies in glass cases, wings spread and pinned with needles.

"Has she . . . collected any new ones lately?" I heard myself ask.

Reb nodded vigorously. He didn't have much in the way of a neck, so he more or less nodded his whole upper body. "Just this morning. The first of this long year," he explained. "A great catch, oh, yes. Half the city's been to see it."

I looked at Reb in some confusion. What was a long year? A queenfest? One thing came through crystal-clear, though. They had caught something that morning. And I was afraid the catch was Peter.

"Where is he?" I burst out.

Reb looked confused. "Who?"

"My . . ." I stopped myself from saying *brother*. I took a deep breath. "I mean, the . . . the queen-people boy. The one they caught."

"In Crystal Hall, of course," Reb said. "Where else would they put it?"

"Take us there," I said with more confidence than I knew I had.

Reb backed away from me in alarm. "Oh, no," he said. "Not good, not good at all, oh, no. Does it *want* to be bones?"

It took me a moment to realize he meant me.

"I'm a girl, Reb," I explained. "Not an *it*."

There was a puzzled pause. Then he politely repeated:

"Does girl want to be bones?" he asked.

I gave up on the grammar lesson. "No," I said, "But I need to see him. It. Whatever. I need to see this . . . catch."

"Bad waters to swim in," Reb cried. "Bad waters for girl. Oh, yes. Very dangerous."

"Taranee, maybe we shouldn't go without—" began Will, but I had no time for objections.

"If you won't take me there, I'll go alone," I said to Reb. "Just point me in the right direction."

Again, there was a moment of puzzled silence. Then he lifted one hand and pointed downward. There was a giggle from Irma.

"Okay, then, Taranee. Off you go!" she said. "Great directions."

I gave her an irritated glance. Then I turned back to Reb.

"I need more than that," I told him, trying to be patient. "You have to tell me exactly how to get there."

He shook his head violently, a movement that, like his nods, involved most of the top half of his body. "Bad waters," he repeated.

"I get that," I said. "If you won't tell me, I'll just ask someone else."

I glared at him. He looked back sullenly. His eyes were a dark golden color, flecked with black.

"Girl won't listen," he hissed. "Girl have bones. Maybe Reb has bones, too."

I didn't say anything. I just kept up the glaring. Finally he sighed and ducked his head.

"Bones," he muttered. "Bones and bad waters. But Reb knows a way into the hall. A darkwater way. Almost hidden. Spinies don't go there, oh, no."

"Take us," I pleaded.

He gave a fluid shrug. Then he moved toward one of the three pipe openings branching out from the junction we were in. "Reb will show you. Girl follow," he said, and slithered into the pipe.

Irma cast a suspicious eye at the path he wanted us to take. "Can we trust him?" she whispered. "Maybe there's a reward or something. For catching queen people. And the spiny thing called him a thief."

"Who else have we got?" I said.

"I like him," said Will. "I think he's kind of cute."

"You like anything that looks like a frog," said Irma with some exasperation. Which is true—Will has frog slippers, frog posters, frog towels, frog pencils, a frog alarm clock, and about a zillion stuffed frogs of every shape, size, and description. She's a frogaholic.

Reb poked his head back out. "Girl coming?" he asked.

"Yeah," I said. "We're coming."

8

I don't know how long or far down we walked. There were spots along the way where we could breathe fresh air. The rest of the time, Irma's magic created air bubbles for us that were almost like divers' helmets. Without her, we would never have survived the long, dark, downward trip.

We paused for breath in an air bell anchored above a rusty two-way path. Below us, frog people and Spinies glided by, hanging on to something that reminded me of a primitive ski lift. The air in the bell was stale, and the floor was covered with trash. The glass walls were nearly opaque with algae and other crud.

"Look," said Reb, pointing downward. "Crystal Hall."

I think I had expected some kind of submarine castle, perhaps because this was what Reb called the "queen place." It looked nothing like a castle. It was more like a huge, floating pinball machine, full of curved tubes and colored lights and slots through which people—frog people and Spinies alike—were constantly emerging.

"Reb," I said, lightly touching one of his smooth-skinned arms, "what are those green lights?"

He gave me one of his do-stupid-girls-know-anything-at-all looks. I had been getting quite a number of those.

"Merefire," he said. "I told you, it's the queen place. That's where they make it."

"Why do they keep the . . . the queen people there?" I asked.

There came another inquisitive look, this one a bit more speculative. "Queen not like them," he said. "Queen especially not like queen people who can make Truefire!" His eyes darted about, as if he were making sure there were no unseen listeners. But this situation made Reb nervous.

"Well, that's going to make *you* very popular, isn't it?" Irma said to me. "Want to pop in and say hello to Her Majesty while we're down there?"

"*No!*" he hissed, and then he exploded in a series of the clicks and nervous tones he'd used with the Spinies. It took him a while to recover his ability to speak, and when he did, he was nearly incoherent.

"Mustn't! Mustn't!" Reb sputtered out. "Oh, no, bones in the water, girl mustn't do that!"

"She didn't mean it," I said, trying to soothe him. "She often says things she doesn't mean."

"Bad! Very bad!" Reb said. "Why girl do that?"

"It was a joke," said Irma helplessly.

"Bad joke. Oh, yes. Very bad joke."

"I agree with Reb," said Will, with a little smile at Irma.

Irma pouted. "You're about as much fun as a wet blanket on a cold day," she said, making Reb almost cross-eyed with bafflement.

"Wet blanket?" he muttered. "Wet blanket a bad joke, too?"

"Sort of," I said. "Why doesn't the queen like Truefire?"

"Don't know, don't know." He hesitated, then cautiously said: "Could be because of the song. Oh, yes, could be." His mouth stretched in what could only have been a grin, and he began to sing:

Truefire, Truefire,
All burn down.
Burn them Spinies out of town.

Truefire, Truefire,
Hot and keen,
Soon no Spinies, soon no queen.

After he had finished singing, he looked at me. And then he said, very solemnly, "Have you come to burn the Spinies, Truefire Girl?"

The hope in his eyes was almost unbearable. I suddenly realized how much his people feared the Spinies. But I couldn't lie to him. That would have been even worse.

"I've come to get my brother back," I said. "Anything else is . . . incidental."

He slowly closed his golden eyes, and for a moment he looked so sad that I wanted to hug him, flippers and all.

"Got to go the darkwater way, now," he said after a while, sounding tired and afraid. "Girl stay close. Not a nice way, oh, no."

Reb was right. His darkwater way was not nice at all. Most of the water went through narrow, dirt-encrusted pipes, some with a bit of air in them, some not. The water that flowed sluggishly around us was filthy, too, clogged with all sorts of refuse.

Finally, we came to a rusty grate that was bent.

"Big breath," said Reb. "Long time no air. Swim for the light."

He dived into the narrow opening and maneuvered his slim body past the grate. I eyed the gap suspiciously. Would we even be able to follow?

"Bend the bars a bit more," suggested Will. Then she added with a smile, "Truefire Girl."

She was right. I nodded, and the water began to boil around the metal rods, turning red like the wire in an old-fashioned toaster. Using fire in water is not easy, and I was panting with the strain before I had finished. I was finally able to grab the grate and bend it while the iron was still soft.

"Nice job," said Irma.

"Thanks," I said. "And now it's your turn again, Irma. There's no way even a very big breath will be enough to get us through this one."

"I'll keep us breathing," she promised.

"Let's go," said Will. "Might as well get it over with. I don't like this place, but I think I'll hate the next one even more."

Nothing more to be said, nothing more to be done.

Knowing it would not be enough, I took a deep breath, and dived for the gap.

The light we were heading for was a mere pin-point at first, easy to miss.

When we burst out at the other end, Reb had already wrestled aside the grate. With a slick twist and heave, he was through the hole and into the room above. We followed and found ourselves in a low-ceilinged room that was crammed with barrels and nets. Thankfully, it was deserted.

We rested a short while and then headed for the trapdoor at one end of the room.

"Crystal Hall. Be very quiet now," hissed Reb. "Or Spinies will hear us."

Inch by inch he eased open the trapdoor and then slipped through it. We followed.

Color. Lights. People. Noise. It was a shock after the long time in the dimness of Reb's dark-water way. The vast hall was crowded with wad-dling frog people and Spinies, some bearing the crown badge. Others, apparently, were just ordi-nary Stromtown citizens. Many had children in tow. A small frog boy was yelling to his mother that he wanted to go on the air slide again. All the children were clutching floating spheres of Merefire that bobbed at the end of strings. The spheres were casting a sickly green glow on everyone's faces. I shuddered. There was something about Merefire that felt so *twisted*, so completely wrong.

"How can they use *that* for a toy?" I muttered.

"Not toy," he said. "Without Merefire, no light, no heat for cooking. All come here to get it every quartyear, even those on the pipeweb, oh, yes, because bringing it home is the task of the children."

"Why?" I asked.

He shrugged. "Just is. It's the queenfest."

"Queenfest?" Irma asked.

He looked completely taken aback, like a child encountering somebody who has never heard of Christmas. "You have no queenfests?"

We all shook our heads.

He touched my arm gently. "Sorry for girl."

"But Reb . . ." said Will. "Why aren't you at this queenfest, then?"

"Don't want no part of queenfest," he said, defiantly. But it was clear that he longed to be one of those children, proudly carrying home the family's supply of Merefire. After a pause, he added: "Got to pay tax. Got to say you love the queen, or you don't get any. Reb's mama don't do that. Reb's mama got pride!"

So did Reb's mama's child, obviously. Will patted him awkwardly on the shoulder.

"Got to go," he said briskly, shrugging off her hand. "Got to go see the catch."

The catch. My brother.

⬤ ⬤ ◬ ◉ ⬤

"Don't let it slip this time," I whispered at Irma. "With all these Spinies about, we'll be in deep trouble if they realize we're not frog people!"

"Have a little faith," she muttered as she struggled to use her magic to protect her.

Unnoticed, we threaded our way through the crowd, steering clear of all Spinies and in particular of those wearing the crown badge. There were several signs saying: DISPLAY ROOM. Most of the crowd was heading that way, too, and we had to stand in line for what seemed like forever before we were allowed through.

In the center of the room stood a huge tank. Inside the tank was a glass tube, and inside that was Peter, wearing his blue swimsuit. His eyes were closed, and he seemed to be asleep.

The Spinies all crowded around. One of them drew a talon slowly down the side of the glass tank, making a screeching sound.

"Taranee, *don't!*" hissed Will, clutching my hands. It was only then I realized that I had raised them. I wanted to set fire to something.

"Get her out of here," said Irma, "before someone notices."

What was there to notice? I wondered, other than my *brother,* stuck in that thing for the Spinies to look at as if he were some lobster in a restaurant fish tank?

Steam, apparently. I was so hot with holding back fire that my wet hair and clothes had begun to steam out of control.

Irma and Will hustled me out of the area. Reb followed, practically hopping in alarm.

"Mustn't make smoke," he hissed.

"Settle *down,* Taranee," said Will in her firmest voice. "We can't do anything now. Not with that crowd of Spinies in there." She turned to Reb. "Does this place close?"

He nodded. "Soon. One more clock hour, maybe two."

"Right," said Will. "We'll do it, then, Taranee. We'll get him out, I promise!"

Irma put a comforting arm around me.

"At least he's asleep," she said. "At least he doesn't know."

9

We went back to the storage space to wait for the right opportunity. I couldn't stop thinking of the Spinies, their fanged grins, and Peter, helplessly asleep. Twice, Reb eased the hatch open, and twice he rapidly closed it again.

"Too many Spinies," he said glumly. "Not good, oh, no."

Finally it was quiet for a long time. There were no more footsteps nor slithering sounds of Spiny tails dragging.

"Now," I said, fed up with waiting. "Let's do it now."

Reb still hesitated.

"Girl," he said. "Please. Can you make Truefire? Just a little. Just to show me, so it will be easier to be brave."

He did look very scared. There was almost

no green left in his face, and his eyes were wide.

I picked up a scrap of frayed rope from the floor and made it catch fire. I held it out to him in my cupped palm, a small bright glow in the dimness of the storage space. Reb gasped, then reached for it.

I stopped him. "Don't. It would hurt you."

Reb had never seen or felt fire, I realized. Had the queen outlawed it?

Reb looked puzzled and disappointed. "Girl don't hurt," he said.

"I have power over fire," I told him. "Trust me, Reb, it would feel bad if you touched it."

He looked at the fire for a long time.

"Reb thought it only burn Spinies," he said at last.

"No," I said. "Other people, too."

"Queens?" he asked.

"Maybe," I answered.

He grinned and then began to sing. "Truefire, Truefire, all burn down," he sang softly. "Burn them Spinies out of town."

The last strands of rope curled into black threads and then into ash. The fire died.

"Can we go now?" I said.

Reb nodded. "Yes. Reb is all brave now, oh, yes."

He looked very small to me, his head only just level with my chest. He was a tiny hero. The bruise on his chest was dark and ugly against his pale skin. But there was a defiant set to his sloping shoulders, and a bright reflection in his golden eyes, as if they still held an echo of the fire.

The display room was empty. Globes of Merefire lit it, but they were dimmer now. The fish in the tank moved more sluggishly, and Peter was still asleep.

"Can't we just smash the glass?" I whispered.

"Bit noisy," murmured Will. "We've got to get into it from above, I think."

There was no obvious way to do that. No handy beams, no chandeliers to swing from. The white tube giving Peter his air came straight out of a hole in the ceiling, and in any case, we had no rope. Then I had an idea.

"Irma," I said. "Ask the water in the tank to *lift* Peter out."

Irma's eyes lit up. "Okay, genius. One brother, coming up."

She raised her hands. Immediately, the water began to heave and boil around the glass tube as it rose slowly to the top of the tank. The water didn't stop there. Pillowed on a determined wave, it slipped over the edge, then dropped to the floor beside us, in a splash of cascading water. The glass didn't break. And Peter didn't show any signs of waking up.

I tensed, ready to deal with any Spinies drawn by the noise. None showed.

Will was staring at the tube. "It doesn't look very breakable," she said. "And there's no lid or hinges or anything like that. How do we open it?"

"With fire," I said. "I'll melt the glass."

"Without scalding Peter?" Will asked.

I nodded. "I'll contain it." I said it with more certainty than I felt, because not many things in the natural world are hotter than melted glass. But I didn't see any other way to get Peter out. I put my hands on the spot by his feet and concentrated.

The glass went cloudy for a moment, and then it began to glow and bubble. But it didn't melt the way it was supposed to. The glass case exploded.

Shards went flying everywhere, lethally sharp. Suddenly, it was hard to breathe. A terrible stench assaulted my nose and mouth, heavy and noxious. I retched, but it provided no relief. My head felt all funny, and it started to droop. Why was I on my knees? I didn't have time to sit down. Peter. Was Peter all right? I needed . . . I needed . . . *You need Hay Lin to blow away this gas,* a cool little voice in my head said. But Hay Lin wasn't there. A siren was blasting away at my eardrums, and from above us, something dropped—a net, a web of Merefire. I think I screamed.

In a flash, the room was full of Spinies. And someone else. The queen.

The queen's hair was silvery white and long enough to coil about her waist. A diamond crown rested on her head, studded with green gems. And the gown that hugged her slim form was woven entirely out of green Merefire. How could she bear its touch? The filament that lay across my shoulders and neck was searing my skin like dry ice, yet she seemed entirely unaffected by that, or by the gas that was slowly clearing in the room.

"So," she said, in a tone of immense satisfaction. "The mouse took the cheese. I am so pleased. Do you want to fight me, Guardian? Please do try. I haven't had this much fun in centuries."

I did try. I struggled to raise one hand.

Fire, I begged silently. Burn. Burn this web away, and burn that smug smile off her face!

A weak smoldering flickered along the edge of my hand for a moment, then died. The queen laughed.

"See?" she told the Spinies massed around us. "That's all there is to this so-called Truefire. No threat at all."

One of the Spinies, by far the biggest I had yet seen, eyed us speculatively.

"Attack?" it asked.

"No, Hallud, not yet," the queen replied. "Perhaps not at all. It depends how stubborn they are. You see, I have a small task for them to do. Oh, Hallud, do you know how long I have been waiting for this?" She smiled warmly, and for a moment looked like a young girl going off to her first big party.

Then I realized. This was the sorceress herself. I knew that as surely as I knew the painful touch of the Merefire.

"Dear Guardian," she purred. "So kind of you to come."

I couldn't bear it. If I had been a dragon, I could have breathed fire at her. Instead, I closed my eyes and tried to make her hair catch on fire.

Slash. A hot-and-cold line of Merefire across one cheek punished me for my mental attack. Then a Spiny foot came down on my chest, hard enough to knock the breath out of me.

"Ressspect," hissed the Spiny called Hallud. "Ressspect for Her Mhajesssty the queen!" He drew back a spined fist for a blow, but the queen stopped him.

"That will do, Hallud," she said.

I looked at her hair. It was barely singed. What was happening to me? I should have had her silver wig blazing by then. Was it the gas? I couldn't seem to think straight, couldn't seem to concentrate. Irma and Will looked just as stunned, and Peter was still slumped on the floor, unconscious among the shards of the broken tube. The Merefire was eating at my skin like acid. I wanted to roll in pain, but that would only have made it worse.

"Take them to the chamber," said the queen. "It's time to begin."

10

The Spinies put Merefire nets around us and started to lead us to the chamber.

"Wait," I said. "My brother . . ."

"All in good time," said the queen. "Don't worry, Guardian. He shall join you soon!"

Spinies hustled us along, apparently impervious to the touch of the Merefire that still bound us. I could think of no way to resist them, but when I realized where they were taking us, hope and fear flared in me at once. The maelstrom chamber. Cornelia and Hay Lin. Would they be able to help us? Would we have a chance to break free?

No chance. On the sandy cave floor, my two friends already waited, tied just as we were with strands of the hateful Merefire.

"Are you all right?" said Will.

Hay Lin hung her head.

"We tried to fight her," she said. "But we . . . it didn't seem to work right. Maybe she's just too strong."

"Maybe we never should have gone near her in the first place," said Cornelia. "Maybe we should have agreed on a sensible plan, instead of *some* of us storming off on our own."

"You didn't want to come!" I snapped.

"You didn't *want* me to!" Cornelia retorted.

"I never said that," I replied.

"Stop it," said Will, looking exhausted.

"Look, just . . . just stop fighting, can't you?" Will pleaded.

Cornelia glared at me, her face pale with anger and fear. I glared back. Then I slumped to the floor, trying to find a way to sit that kept the Merefire off my skin. What was wrong with us? Ever since we had come to this place, it was as if we couldn't agree on even the simplest things.

And then I froze, sitting completely still. Our fighting hadn't started until we had gotten to this place. The fighting had begun the exact moment the Heart had been broken.

"Will," I whispered, almost afraid to voice my thought. "Let me see the Heart for a moment."

She raised her head. "What for?"

"Just . . ." I began to explain. "Just something I want to check."

"It's still broken," Will whispered.

"I'd just like a look at it," I pleaded. "Please, Will?"

She shrugged, and brought out the Heart. Then she gasped.

"It's worse! Taranee," she cried.

Will was right. The twist was longer, darker, uglier. It went clean through the crystal, dividing the orb into two unequal halves.

"It's us," I said. "We're broken, because the Heart is. That's why we're fighting all the time. That's why nothing works as well as it does when we're together."

Will looked as if she were about to break in half herself.

"It's my fault," she whispered, "I was supposed to look after the Heart."

"It's not your fault," said Irma.

When I looked over at Cornelia, I was still feeling mad. My temper rose inside me like a fire burning. I tried to control my feelings.

This isn't right, this isn't real, I thought. Cornelia is one of my five best friends.

I held out my hand to Cornelia. "I'm sorry, and I wish we were best friends again," I said, solemnly, with all my heart.

She stared at me. I had surprised her.

"Think about it," I urged her. "Remember what the Oracle said? The wish of a Guardian is a powerful force. For good or ill. Wish me well, Cornelia. Heal the Heart."

"You *are* nuts," Cornelia said.

"No, she's not," said Will suddenly. "Can't you feel it? We're not whole. We're broken. Taranee is right—we can heal. If we want to."

"It's a crystal," Cornelia said. "You can't heal a crystal."

"You *know* it's not just a crystal," Will said. "It's—"

"Quiet," hissed Hay Lin. "All of you. She's coming!"

The queen entered the chamber. At her heels came Hallud, with Peter, who was slung over his shoulder, still unconscious. The queen was smiling. Around her, Merefire spun and twined, in her hair, at her throat, around her hands. The sullen maelstrom in the basin seemed to swirl faster and colder in her presence.

"Now," she said, glittering in anticipation, "*now* I shall finally have my rightful place. And you shall give it to me!"

I had no idea what she was talking about, but

inside me, something had begun to tremble with fear. She looked very powerful. She glowed with whirling and twisting Merefire.

"Bring me the Guardian," she said. She gestured in my direction, and most of my Merefire strands melted away. Hallud dumped Peter onto the floor and grabbed my arm.

"Kneel," he hissed.

I didn't want to, but I was afraid of what might happen to Peter, to all of us, if I didn't.

She gazed down at me. "For your own sake," she said, "I hope you are a very good Guardian. The task I set for you is not for the weak. But if you do not solve it, I have no further use for you—or for your brother. Do I make myself clear?"

Numbly, I nodded. I truly believed that she would harm us.

"What is it you want me to do?" I managed to say.

Her smile broadened. "When I first came here, there was nothing, just the rocks and the sea. That was all. It took me a long time to learn how to draw things to me, through the stromatolite. Everything here is mine. Even these creatures—" She gestured at the Spinies and at Reb. "Even these are mine. If not for me, they wouldn't exist."

"Not true," Reb said quietly. It was a very small, defiant whisper, but it stopped the queen.

"What did you say?" she asked, turning her menacing stare on Reb. "You dare to speak in my presence?"

Reb wasn't looking at her. He was looking straight at me.

"Truefire Girl," he said, fearfully, but with stubborn pride. "We are not hers."

"If not for me you'd still be hopping and croaking and snatching at flies!" the queen barked.

"We are not hers," repeated Reb quietly. "We are our own people. We have our own lives, our own stories, our own dreams. We made this Stromtown, as much as she did. But she became afraid that we would grow disobedient, and so she brought the Spinies, and set them loose on us. Since then we have lived in fear. They are strong and ruthless, and we are weaker and more timid. Courage does not come easy to our kind."

The queen sent a bolt of Merefire in Reb's direction. It hit him squarely in the middle of his bruised chest and he was hurled back against the cavern wall. He slid to the floor and lay still.

I had raised my hands without even thinking about it. But the spinning circle at my throat tightened like a noose, so that for a few long moments I couldn't even breathe.

"Careful, Guardian," hissed the queen. "I am stronger than you are."

She was right. She *was* strong. However she had initially come by her magic, she had much more of it now. Perhaps, if I had spent a few centuries brooding and hoarding power, I'd be just as strong.

"If you're so strong," I croaked painfully, the Merefire rope still tight around my throat, "how come you need me?"

That didn't please her. For a moment, the rope tightened still further, and darkness threatened to overwhelm me. When air and light came back, I was on my hands and knees in the sand next to Peter.

"There is this little thing," the queen said. "This little thing I can't do. You see, I can draw things in through the stromatolite. But much as I've tried, I have not been able to pass myself back out through it. So that is your task, Guardian: send me back. Then you and your friends can stay here and spoil the froggies to your hearts' content."

11

"I . . . I need my friends," I said to the queen, buying more time. "I can't do this alone."

"You have them," she growled. "They're here."

"No, I mean, with me," I said. "We need to be able to touch."

The queen looked suspicious, but then she nodded. With a quick motion of her hand, she freed the others from most of their bonds, leaving them with just Merefire collars like mine.

"How do we do this?" I asked, searching their faces desperately for some answer, some way out of this.

"We can't," whispered Hay Lin frantically, trying not to let the queen hear her. "We *can't* let that . . . that twisted monster back into our universe."

"If we don't, she'll—" began Cornelia, but Will interrupted her.

"Wait," Will said. "I think we should do what she wants."

"What?" I was taken aback. "Will, you can't be serious!"

"It's the only way out," Will said, with a peculiar emphasis. "Remember? Trust your heart. An ancient wrong may be put right."

She was quoting the Oracle, I realized. And a small light dawned in my brain. If Will was right . . . if we could somehow untwist the maelstrom and get reconnected to the rest of the universe. . . .

"What if you're wrong?" I whispered, hardly daring to speak the words.

Will just looked at me. Her face was still pale, but she was looking better than she had at any time since the Heart had broken.

"Trust me," she said. "Wish me well. Heal the Heart."

And she brought the Heart into her palm.

"What are you doing?" asked the queen, raising a menacing hand. "Don't try anything sneaky. You'll only regret it."

"Don't you want to go back?" said Will, innocently. "The Heart can send you. It's the only thing that can. You've got to trust me."

Grudgingly, the Queen nodded. "Do it, then," she said. "I've waited long enough."

Will looked at each of us in turn. "Now," she said. "You, too, Cornelia."

Cornelia hesitated for a long moment.

"Okay," she finally said. "Let's try."

Will held out the broken Heart. It was painful to look at the fractured orb, and I quickly put my hand on top of Will's, hiding the flaw. When we look at it again, I firmly told myself, it will be beautiful and shining and *whole* again. Hay Lin's hand joined mine.

"Now you," said Irma to Cornelia. "And I'll go last."

Cornelia's hand came to rest on top of Hay Lin's. Irma's followed. And we all closed our eyes and *wished*, with all our strength. I wanted to be whole. I didn't want to fight and quarrel all the time. I wanted all of us to be well, and to be safe, including Reb and Peter.

At first, nothing happened. Then a gentle heat began seeping from the crystal into our hands, a pulsing heat, like a heartbeat, slow and stumbling at first, then stronger and stronger. It went through all of us. Water. Fire. Air. Earth. Energy.

White light washed through the chamber, drowning out the green glare of the Merefire. From the Spiny guards came a squawk of surprise, and the queen took a stumbling step back.

"Put that away," she bellowed at me. "Put it out, or I'll make sure that you never see your brother again!"

"You wanted to go back," said Will. "Your wish is about to come true."

The Heart was whole. I could both see it and feel it. And Will was herself again, strong and confident.

"Now," Will said, "this time we do it differently. This time we take this thing apart." She nodded at the maelstrom. "Taranee, it has fire in it. Get that fire. Irma, it has water, too. You get that. Untwist it. Make the element pure."

If only, I thought, I could make this type of fire remember what fire should be—clean, hot, and impatient, not some murky, green, unnatural stuff.

Slowly, I let my hand sink into the swirling maelstrom. *Come*, I called to the trapped fire. *Come. I'll show you how to burn.* My hand hurt, but I kept at it. I could feel Will giving me strength. I could feel Hay Lin, Cornelia, and Irma, busy with their own hard tasks.

The maelstrom flickered uncertainly. So did the Merefire bonds holding us. We're doing it, I thought. We're really doing it! Little flames of fire—Truefire—licked at my hands now. After the Merefire, it was like being touched by a friend. From Irma's side of the basin, steam rose from the swirling water.

"No!" cried the queen furiously. "Not like that! Hallud, stop them!"

But the big Spiny guard stood frozen, staring at the fire flowing up my arms. Then the queen ran at us, shrieking. She looked different, I dimly noted. Smaller. Weaker. Less glittery.

Will's hand shot out and grabbed the queen by the wrist. "Now!" she called. "Into the maelstrom. All of us!"

All of us? But what about Peter? Reb?

There wasn't time to hesitate. "Trust me," Will had said. And I did.

Just touching the Strom had hurt. This was beyond pain. White. Black. Green. Burning cold. Freezing heat. Fire—dark old fire—trapped and corrupted. Water, tainted and warped.

I heard Will's voice.

"Don't fight it," Will said. "Just show it how to be free."

The fire had been twisted and trapped for

centuries. It wanted to burn clean. I showed it how. Stromtown would never be the same.

There was silence. Beyond my closed eyelids, there was light. Gently I floated up. I could have stayed that way for ages, just savoring the peace, the *rightness* of it all.

"Taranee."

Reluctantly, I opened my eyes. A vast, pillared hall. A space so huge it looked almost infinite. And in the midst of it, the Oracle. He was smiling.

"Welcome," the Oracle said.

"Thank you," I murmured, wondering if there were a polite way of asking whether I was still alive. Then I noticed the others. Will, Irma, Cornelia, and Hay Lin. The queen and even Peter, who was still unconscious, were there.

The queen no longer looked royal or powerful. Every trace of Merefire was gone. Instead of her bright, shining gown, she wore a simple linen shift. Her hair was thin and scraggly, and though her face was still unlined, her skin looked lifeless and papery. But the most striking thing was her power, or rather, the lack of it. All the glitter had gone. What was left was . . . what had the Oracle said? A young girl with a touch of magic.

I looked at Will. "Did you know?" I asked.

"Did you know that if we brought her back into the proper world, she'd lose her powers?"

Will smiled faintly. "I hoped so. I trusted my heart, like the Oracle told us to."

"You have done well," the Oracle decreed. "You are indeed worthy Guardians."

"Thank you," I said again, bowing my head slightly. "Um . . . is everything all right now?"

The Oracle nodded and then explained. "What was trapped has been freed. What was twisted has been made right. The sorceress will face the judgment of the Congregation, and you may return to your world with your brother."

I was relieved, but then I had another concern. "What about Reb?" I asked. "What about his people? And the Spinies?"

"The fate of any world belongs to its people," the Oracle said.

"But can you see them now?" I urged the Oracle to tell us. "Are those creatures still there?"

"I see them," the Oracle confirmed. "Their world is again part of my infinity. But there is no longer a passageway from your world into theirs."

"Can't I at least say good-bye?" I asked. "I don't even know if Reb is okay." He had hit that wall awfully hard for someone so small.

"Very well," the Oracle said. "But don't be long."

12

I found Reb sitting on a rock, watching the sunrise. He looked tired and bruised, but otherwise all right.

"Did you burn queen?" he asked.

"Um . . . not exactly. But she's gone. She won't bother you again." I sat down beside him on the rock.

He nodded, and took a contented sigh. Then he frowned. "Spinies are still here, though."

"This is their world now, too," I told him. "You'll have to work something out."

"Mmmm." He looked doubtful.

"Reb," I said. "I just came to say good-bye."

He looked at me sideways. "Girl can't go," he said. "Need you."

I shook my head, and the beads in my braids made a clicking sound. "I can't stay. I don't belong here. And I need to go home."

Reb looked away. "But girl is the only one who can do the magic. We need that. Need the Truefire."

I understood Reb's situation. And suddenly I realized that I had the power to help him.

"Who says I'm the only one who can do magic?" I said. "Reb, give me a few of those reeds—dry, please. And take these." I took off my glasses and handed them to him. "Look, hold them just like this." I positioned my glasses so that the sun was shining directly onto the lenses. "That little white sunspot there—keep it on the reeds. And wait."

It took a while. Maybe even a bit longer than it would have done at home. But after a while the reeds started to blacken. And suddenly, a small bright flame leaped up.

Reb sprang to his feet. "Look! I made Truefire. Look!"

I smiled. "Yes. You did."

"Them Spinies won't dare mess with Reb now, oh, no! Reb can make Truefire, just like girl!" Then he suddenly stopped his prancing. "But Truefire glasses are yours," he said.

"Keep them," I said. My mother would scold me. At least, she would once she got over the joy of having Peter back home.

"I really have to go now," I said, getting up. I gave Reb a careful, damp hug. He clung to me for a moment.

"Don't want you to go," he said.

"You've got the Truefire now," I said. "You'll have to be responsible. Fire can be dangerous, too."

"I know," he said, and gave me a tight squeeze.

He let go of me slowly, and watched me go back down the stairs. When I was quite sure he couldn't hear me, I cleared my throat.

"Um, I'm ready to go home now," I said to the unseen Oracle, not sure how I would get there.

The rest is pretty much a blur—literally. I really don't see very well without my glasses. The Oracle brought me back to the others and then returned us all to Heartbreak Island.

"Farewell for now, Guardians," the Oracle said. "Stay true to the Heart."

In the boat on the way back to Pleasance, Peter finally started to wake up. He looked very confused.

"Taranee?" he said. "Where am I?"

"On your way home," I said.

"My head," he moaned. "What happened?"

"Windsurfing accident," I explained.

"But you . . . but how . . ." he began to ask.

"Shhh," I said. "I think you hit your head or something. You probably shouldn't be talking."

"I've had the weirdest dreams. They were so vivid. I think you were there. And . . . and *frogs*, of all things. Weird, I tell you."

"Dreams are strange," I told him, trying to keep a straight face.

He managed a small grin. "Serves me right, though, doesn't it? For standing you up the other night."

"*No*, it doesn't," I said. "You didn't deserve this. I never wished you ill. Never."

He looked surprised. "Easy. I never thought you did."

"Good," I said, blinking away a few tears. "Because I didn't. I love you, and I *never* want to lose you again."

"Whoa," he said. "What brought that on?" Then he softened. "I love you, too. And next week, we'll go see the Hawks together. I promise."

His eyes started to droop again, and he slept for the rest of the way back to Pleasance. I held his hand, so happy to have him back that it made my chest hurt. Will gave me a small smile.

I looked over at Hay Lin and Irma, who were busy working air and water to keep our boat moving, and at Cornelia, who was sitting next to Will. It felt so nice to have the Heart whole again, to have us whole. When the Heart was broken, it had been the worst kind of heartbreak. Now, with the orb all in one piece, we—W.I.T.C.H.— were whole again. A true team. And that was a slam-dunk feeling.